The Tickle Tree

Written by Chae Strathie a...

Have you ever been there
where the Tickle Tree grows...

...and laughed as it jiggles its twigs on your toes?.

Have you sat on the back of a giant galumph

and let out a 'whoop' as you slid down its hump?

4

Have you scratched an old crabbysnap under its chin

or slept through the sound of a boomjangle's din?

Have you walked with a wibblebird made out of jelly

or perched on the paunch of a blubbalub's belly?

If the answer is **no,**
then you shouldn't despair,
as I'm sure that there's some way
for you to get there.

Have you leapt like a springbungle up to the stars and said "howdy-do!" to the Grimbles on Mars?

Have you wondered why horse-riding

Or played hide and seek with a luminous frink?

poo-munkles stink?

To get there is simple,
but you'll have to wait
and hope that I tell you
before it's too late!

Have you given a moonjack a ride on your foot,
or cuddled a clumph and been hugged by a snoot?

If the answer is no, then that's really tough luck.
Without clear directions it looks like you're stuck.

Have you danced with a **marvellous** musical meep

or dunked with a dennyfish

down in the **deep?**

Have you had a **pink** puffalunk's last piece of pie or climbed a free **fangdangle** up to the sky?

Don't tell me
you haven't,
I'm really surprised.

All right then,
I'll show you, but first
close your eyes.

It's clear that you're eager to get to this place.

Where snugglebugs buzz and ripunzelruns race.

19

I'll show you the way, but it's not where it seems.

Through the Tickle Tree's leaves and . . .

20

...into your dreams!

With love to my mum Gill
and my dad Calum
and not forgetting Eilidh,
who's at the heart of every book.

C.S.

For my children,
who teach me how to fly...

P.B.

The Tickle Tree
Text Copyright | Chae Strathie
Illustration Copyright | Poly Bernatene
The rights of Chae Srathie and Poly Bernatene
to be named as the author and illustrator of
this work have been asserted by them in
accordance with the Copyright, Designs and
Patents Act, 1988

Published in 2016 by Hutton Grove
An imprint of Bravo Ltd.
Sales and Enquiries:
Kuperard Publishers & Distributors
59 Hutton Grove, London, N12 8DS

Tel: +44 (0)208 446 2440
Fax: +44 (0)208 446 2441
sales@kuperard.co.uk
www.kuperard.co.uk

Published by arrangement with Albury Books
Albury Court, Albury, Oxfordshire, OX9 2LP

ISBN 978-1-857338-21-8 (paperback)

A CIP catalogue record for this book
is available from the British Library

10 9 8 7 6 5 4 3
Printed in China